This book belongs to:

A Production of
FoxtaleBooks Publishing

Marvin Kirchner
Plutone Artstation

Kirchheimer Str.81
73265 Dettingen u.Teck
Germany

Illustrations &
Artistic Design
Marvin Kirchner

Text & Production
**Marvin Kirchner
Carolin Kirchner**

Translation & Editing
Carolin Kirchner

1st Edition 2023
**© 2023 Plutone Artstation
© 2023 Foxtale Books**

ISBN Paperback: **9798863269351**
Text © 2023 Marvin Kirchner

For more information,
visit **www.foxtale-books.com**

FOXTALE
BOOKS

For our brave little heroine E.,
who took the big step of giving up
her pacifier.
With love, C. & M.

FOXTALE
BOOKS

FREDDIE
MUST SAY GOODBYE TO HIS PACIFIER

Marvin Kirchner | Carolin Kirchner

Effortlessly Say Goodbye to the Pacifier.
It Can Be That Easy!

Once upon a time, there was a little bear named Freddie, whose best friend was a little pacifier. From the very beginning, he was a very calm and content bear. Even as a little baby, Freddie had his pacifier in his mouth. It went with him everywhere and made sure that Freddie felt safe and secure.

... while playing in the garden,

... in his room,

... while riding in the car,

... and of course, while sleeping.

One night, he had a special dream. He found himself in a forest full of pacifiers and he couldn't get enough of all the different shapes and colours. He walked through the forest and collected as many pacifiers as he could carry.

It was a wondrous place and Freddie was very happy...

A tree full of pacifiers!

The next morning, Freddie told his mama about his dream. "I dreamed about a forest full of binkies," he said excitedly. **"It was so nice!"**

But then Freddie's mama said something to him that Freddie hadn't expected:

"Freddie, my darling, it's time to say 'goodbye' to your pacifier. Look, at home and in the bear kindergarten, you don't need it anymore. You are now a big, brave bear. It's time to fall asleep without your pacifier."

Mama Bear added: "You know, the pacifier is not good for your little bear teeth either. And we want you to be healthy and strong, my little Freddie."

Freddie was worried about how he should fall asleep without his binky. He sighed. "But how will I manage that?"

Freddie was very unhappy that he now had to give up the pacifier even for sleeping. It also made him angry because he couldn't imagine it without him. It helped him fall asleep and gave him a feeling of security.

Mama Bear compassionately told him that it was perfectly normal to be mad and angry when you have to part with something that means so much to you.
She stood by Freddie and encouraged him to overcome this challenge.

GRRRRR!!!

Luckily, Freddie's Papa had a **brilliant idea.** He gave Freddie a little box to paint, in which he could place his pacifier.

With the hearty support of Mama and Papa Bear, Freddie created a charming pacifier box, colourfully painted...

...and adorned with lots of love.

Freddie felt courage and bravery welling up inside him. That evening, he carefully placed his beloved pacifier into the box. His little bear heartbeat uncertainly, but Mama Bear was by his side. She smiled at him and snuggled with him into his soft bear bed.

Freddie's Pacifier Box

That night, Freddie fell fast asleep without his pacifier...

... He dreamed of an **enchanted forest** that was so mysterious and magical, Freddie felt like a brave explorer, ready to discover everything. It was an exciting adventure that Freddie would remember for a long time.

hu-hu-hu

When the first sunbeams tickled Freddie's face the next morning, he woke up feeling lively. Now it was time to get ready for bear kindergarten. And the pacifier box? It had completely slipped his mind in the excitement of the morning.

Little Freddie spent an exciting day at kindergarten. While playing and laughing with his friends, he forgot everything around him.

Freddie the Pirate!

When it was time to go home, he felt
happy and secure, and that was all
without his pacifier.

"Mama," he said proudly. "I think I can manage to fall asleep without a pacifier."

"I'm so happy to hear that, my dear," said his mama and gave him a kiss on the cheek. "You are so brave and strong."

"But what are we going to do with the pacifier box now?" Freddie asked curiously..

"That's for you to decide," Mama Bear answered with a smile.

Freddie thought for a moment. "I want **to bury the box in the garden.** That way, I can always remember how big I've become and how I gave up my pacifier."

Freddie was full of anticipation as he began to dig a hole in the garden. It was an important step for him and a sign that he was now a big bear who no longer needed his pacifier.

When he finally placed the box into the hole and carefully filled it in, he was very proud of himself. Freddie knew that he was now ready to experience new adventures. All without his pacifier!

Adress:
Bear Baby Hospital
in Bear Town
on Brown Bear Street 12

Freddie lit up at the thought. Together with Mama Bear, he carefully packed all his remaining pacifiers into a colourful little parcel. In big letters, they wrote: "**Bear Baby Hospital**". Freddie was happy that other little bears would now also enjoy his pacifiers.

Full of pride, he told all the other bears in kindergarten about his adventure and inspired them to also say goodbye to their pacifiers.

That evening, Freddie fell asleep peacefully. He had completely forgotten about his pacifier.

Sleep well, little Freddie, and may your dreams be as sweet as a...

...honey cake.

For your parents...

Dear Parents,

You've read the story, and your child is now ready to say goodbye to their pacifier? Fantastic. Then you can create a pacifier box together. Let your creativity run free and choose a small cardboard box or an old lunch box that your child can paint and decorate. Prepare them to place the pacifier into the box before going to bed. The box can be placed in the child's room, the bedroom, or another place.

It's essential that you sensitize your child to the weaning process and explain the importance of saying goodbye to a beloved habit. The book and the homemade pacifier box can help your child take this important step and look forward to a new phase in their life.

We appreciate
a rating and
your feedback

A Production of
FoxtaleBooks Publishing

Illustrations &
Artistic Design
Marvin Kirchner

Text & Production
Marvin Kirchner
Carolin Kirchner

Translation & Editing
Carolin Kirchner

ISBN Paperback: **9798863269351**
© **Marvin Kirchner**
For more information
visit **www.foxtale-books.com**

You are my World
my little sweetheart

16 unique moments of love between mother and child

Marvin Kirchner   Carolin Kirchner

FOXTALE
BOOKS

2+

Explore the variety of our
children's books and visit
us on our website:
www.foxtale-books.com

For our releases
and topics about reading aloud
and helpful guides, follow our
Instagram channel:

foxtale.books.kids

FOXTALE
BOOKS

www.foxtale-books.com

49737585R00022